PAPER MESSAGES

—ANDREA BUFFERT—

PAPER MESSAGES

Volume 2

ReadersMagnet, LLC

Paper Messages: Volume 2
Copyright © 2021 by Andrea Buffert

Published in the United States of America
ISBN Paperback: 978-1-953616-90-6
ISBN eBook: 978-1-953616-91-3

All rights reserved. No part of this publication may be reproduced, stored in a retrieval system or transmitted in any way by any means, electronic, mechanical, photocopy, recording or otherwise without the prior permission of the author except as provided by USA copyright law.

ReadersMagnet, LLC
10620 Treena Street, Suite 230 | San Diego, California, 92131 USA
1.619.354.2643 | www.readersmagnet.com

Book design copyright © 2021 by ReadersMagnet, LLC. All rights reserved.
Cover design by Ericka Obando
Interior design by Shemaryl Tampus

CONTENTS

"God's Creation" 1
"Blooming Flower" 3
From Me To You 5
"Beautiful People" 7
"BARS / WARS" 9
"Message of Love" 11
"YOU" 13
"Don't Bury Me" 15
"Warrior Soldier" 17
"Born Fighters" 19
"PROVIDER" 20
"Who's God" 22
"Text to Sister" 25
"FREE" 27
"God Made it Right" 28
"Happenstance" 31
"My Heart's Desire" 32
"Sweet Release" 34
"OUR ALLOTTED TIME" 36
"YOUR SMILE" 39

"DECISIONS" 41
"I Speak" 43
"Fellowship" 46
"Almost" 49
"Paper Messages" 53
"PRESSURE" 55
"Management" 57
"The Fiftieth Year" 59
"I can't breathe" 61

"GOD'S CREATION"

I get this impression

Deep in my soul

When we look @ God's creation

We can get some stories told.

Let me try to explain :

Do I want to be like a star

Shining so bright,

Bright enough to lead others to "The Light"

Do I want to be a "falling star"

Just the name "falling star" gives a negative notation, But,

even a falling star gives light, it's just short-lived.

When I think of the moon,

I think of a person with the "big head syndrome"

You know all puffed up with pride inside So, I don't wanna be

like the moon.

Wait a minute,

Yes, the moon appears large in size

to the natural eye

But, I thank God for moonlight

During the pitch black darkness of some nights.

"BLOOMING FLOWER"

The Lord up above

Sends down His love

You've been close to His heart

Right from the start

He sees everything

You're under His wing

Never quit, Never surrender

Because God remembers

He remembers the deeds of love that you have done

Along with the souls you won

Yeah, that's right

Do you think God has forgot

How you taught others to fight!!!

This you must understand

My God is not a man.

Right there in your darkest hour

He sees an ever blooming flower.

How can a flower grow in the dark?

Because of the " Light" in your heart

Now, lift high your head

As you hold on to the promises your

God made !!!

And, always, do what God said.

FROM ME TO YOU

Who's there to encourage the encourager

Who extends a helping hand to the Preacher man

I'm here to let you know

God has released angels to your rescue

You must continue to fight the good fight

You've been commissioned by the Ancient of Days

To lead us

To show us the way

Respectively you should never quit, never surrender

You are chosen by God for such a time as this.

God Bless you

Written by Andrea Buffert

"BEAUTIFUL PEOPLE"

Beautiful people jump start each day,

With acts of kindness, or maybe,

By the words they say.

Beautiful people are sent from "GOD"

With one special assignment....

To spread "HIS" love.

Beautiful people have no secrets,

They have nothing to hide, so...

Onward they march,

They may have a few setbacks,

But, they're never defeated.

Beautiful people never quit,

They never surrender, you wanna know why?

Because they believe in the "ONE" true power of the universe.

The "ONE" that put "time" itself in motion.

Beautiful people allow that same "ONE"

To rule over their emotions,

As they do what they have to do,

To advance in their careers without fear.

And, yes, my sister & my brother,

Absolutely, positively, speaking,

You guys are all GOD's beautiful people, You guys have been strategically placed, On this planet called Earth, To do "HIS" bidding, Among the living,

"BARS / WARS"

Your prison may have a visible bar.

Whereas mine may be more of a mental war.

Bars / Wars .....

No matter the approach,

Both of us are being provoked.

So now we must invoke

The presence of "The Ancient of Days",

To come swiftly to our aide.

Since we know He has no respect of persons, Let us not wait

until our situation worsens.

The enemy has clearly drawn the line in the sand, So, my

brother, I wanna know where do you stand?

You see, I've got my sword in my hand.

I intend to finish strong !

But, because I don't need this turning out wrong I sent Judah first.

My bible tells me in Judges 20:18, King James Version Judah shall go up first!!!!

Now we all know that Judah means Praise.

Yes of course both hands do I raise.

Many days before yesterday,

I dispatched "praise" to go ahead of me, To win this war from our enemy.

"MESSAGE OF LOVE"

Hate kills, LOVE heals.

God sent us His only Son

With all the Splendor & Glory from on High He came to tell us

a story, Of how to live & never die.

Hate kills, LOVE heals.

Now this world was so full of sin,

And it had been for a time & time again.

But there was no shame to Jesus game,

Into this world He came,

He was, He is our Spotless Lamb.

Hate kills, LOVE heals.

Now, I have to suppose,

That everyone knows,

He came to be the Delivering Savior of mankind, Once......

for all time.

Hate kills, LOVE heals.

But I want to talk about, the not so obvious, I want to tell you

that Jesus "did not"

run around like a 3 ring circus

He had this unique way of speaking in parables, to convey

His purpose, He let us know, that our redemption, HE would

purchase, Through the shedding of His Blood Never lack in

supply, Always heavy in surplus.

The message of love

Jesus shared through the blood

Hate kills, but LOVE HEALS !!!!!!!

"YOU"

God had a design in mind,

Something that He just had to do,

Nothing was lost, that He had to find,

He merely spoke, and there were you.

You were carefully placed in your mother's womb, Yes, He was

there with the bride & groom, During the insertion of the sperm

for your conception, You see, He was there for your protection.

Because as God spoke your construction,

The enemy commence planning your destruction.

Destruction of "My" daughter....

"No so", spoke the Almighty Father,

She is, shall, & will be,

Always a part of my family line,

Because, "I AM the TRUE VINE"

And she is one of MY branches,

Being nourished by "ME",

And the "HOLY TRINITY".

"DON'T BURY ME"

Verse 1 : Don't bury me

Beneath that dirty dirt

I ain't dead

I'm just injured and hurt

When you stabbed me

With yo tongue of a knife

Ya took my breath away

And ya nearly took my life

Chorus : Don't do it y'all

Don't do it to ya sisters & brothers

Because some of us out there

May never never never recover

Verse 2 : You see,

I was that wounded soldier

And I was on the battle field

But I had to retreat

Giving myself time to heal

While waiting for healing

To take its proper place

I dropped down on my knees

Began to seek His Holy face

"WARRIOR SOLDIER"

The rationale of these few lines

Is simply to encourage you during these trying times

I know that life can be ever so rough

But that's why "He" made you so tough

You see you are one of God's Mighty, Mighty Warriors

That's what He created you for

Brave enough to stand up to our enemy down on your knees

Asking God to open the saint's eyes so that we may see

To see the different strategies

Being used by the enemy,

Constantly

To divert us from our purpose.

I can almost see you now

Weeping & wailing & mourning out to God

Because you truly have a burden to rescue the lost

No matter the cost or demands on your life

You say " if i can lead just one soul to Christ, no matter the

price, then it's worth the sacrifice "

Well, well, My dear sister

God whispered to me just a few minutes ago

To send a text to let you know

How " He "rejoices @ the mention of your name

God calls you His mighty warrior

soldier "w o m a n"

He says on you He can depend

To complete any task that you begin

He says you make Him proud !!!

ANDREA BUFFERT

"BORN FIGHTERS"

As life continues to present challenges,

We always manage to balance it.

We think quietly to ourself

This , soon ,will be under our belt.

So we continue to look ahead

And never will we allow life to knock us dead !

We are born fighters !!!!

"PROVIDER"

Who is your provider ? .....

Mine sits on high

Constantly checking us out

From the sky

Yes, He's up there

Sitting on His throne

Doing what He does best

Being God alone,

All by Himself.

And, He created all

Inclusive of satan

You know, the one who took the great fall.

God has cared for us since the beginning of time Mankind can

be sure We are always on His mind.

Now, can you tell me

Who, is your provider?

Is it Blue Cross?

All State?

Or Jehovah-Jireh?

As for me and my house,

I stand tall to tell

We call Him Master,

And Savior,

And Emanuel.

So, the answer to the question first stated above, Jehovah-Jireh, is

my provider, He's my Father, my love.

"WHO'S GOD"

Question : Who is God ?

Answer :   God forgives our sins

God is my Rock in the weary land

God is my Jehovah Jireh

God is my Strong Deliverer

God is my Way Maker

God is my Strong Strong Deliverer

God is my way in

God is my way out

God is my Provider

God heals our diseases

God redeems us from hell

God saves our lives

God crowns us with love & mercy

God wraps us in goodness

God renews our youth

God makes everything come out right

God puts victims back on their feet

God is sheer mercy & grace

God is rich in love

God is not easily angered

God doesn't endlessly nag & scold

God doesn't hold grudges forever

God doesn't treat us as our sins deserves God doesn't pay us back in full for our wrongs God knows us inside & out

**God doesn't think the way we think

God doesn't work the way we work

God's word does not go back to Him void or empty-handed God's word will do the work He sent them to do

** God's love never quits

God is my strong champion : I was right on the cliff-edge, ready to fall when God grabbed me and held me

* * God is an honest judge

* * God holds me head & shoulders above all who try to pull me down.

God is my Everything

God is my All in All

Pause to catch my breath........

Oh...., I will answer your question, with this question :

" Have I answered your Question ? "

"TEXT TO SISTER"

That certain time of day is here

For me to text my Sister

Whom I love so dear

Just want to let you know

That the God we serve

Will use this little situation

To show you how much He cares

To let you know He's always there

He's there for you with arms open wide

In His word just continue to abide

God will never leave your side.

"FREE"

Feeling boxed in

So I gotta break free

Y should I be bound

When He delivered me

This message that He gave me

Is like solid gold

And one of my assignments

Is to just get it told.

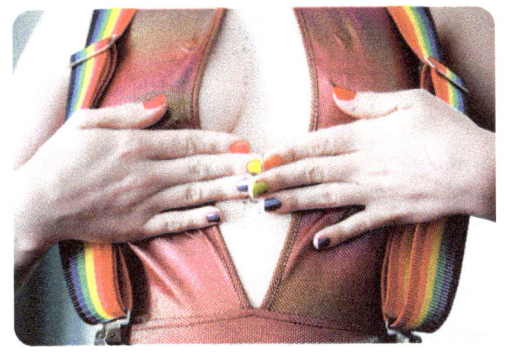

"GOD MADE IT RIGHT"

I do strongly believe

Way back when I was conceived

You see

Right from the start

slew-foot was doing his part

With Mama lying on the sheets

he was planning my defeat

You see

In the beginning

satan thought he was winning

But actually

God had a plan

For each & 'evry human

Planning how He would fill us

With His Holy Spirit

Through

The birth & death of His Son

Known as "The Holy One"

But as

In the beginning

So shall it be in the ending

My God

Will make it right

Um um hmm

God will make it right!

And to this very hour

We still got that Unlimited Power

Why?

Because God made it right

Yeah, yeah, oh yeah

God made it right!

Thank You Jesus

Thank You Jesus

For making it right.

"HAPPENSTANCE"

It's not just happenstance

That I'm facing this particular circumstance

Ain't no coincidence

Because...

I've got the evidence

BUT my GOD won't be negligent

As long as I'm faithful & stay diligent

And the Difference

Will be in the method of DELIVERANCE !!!!!!

"MY HEART'S DESIRE"

I can never get tired

Of my heart's desire

It is an all consuming fire

Keeping me from harm,

Enabling me to discern

And "yes", for "Him" do I yearn.

To stay in "His" presence

Is a MUST.

My "all" with "Him", I trust!

Is it safe to say I speak for all of us?

For protection, "HE is our SHIELD"

But, daily we must yield

Our ways to "HIS WILL"

In "HIM", there is no wrong

In "HIM", we are strong

And always for "HIM",

I do long.

"SWEET RELEASE"

I've been released

Please let me go

I'm all better now

Just look @ me smile !

When my heart was in an awful race

I willingly came to this wonderful place

And, after a cardiac consultation

Doc diagnosed me with atrial fibrillation.

I was admitted for overnight observation

And, yes the good nurses gave me medication.

REST & MEDICATION ,

Stopped the palpitations.

I'm very appreciative for the T.L.C.

That all of your staff have given to me,

But now, you see, I've gotta make haste

I've got to get back to my place!!!

I've been released

Please let me go !

"OUR ALLOTTED TIME"

I am a free moral agent,

So I've been told, "I am free."

Do you see free, when you see me?

Other familiar sayings:

Age is just a number.

You're as young as you feel.

You there, gasping for breath,

As you've just finished your slow morning "walk" up the hill,

Tell me..... How young do you feel?

Too blessed to be stressed!

Really???

We live in a mortal body of flesh.

This flesh is aging daily.

As mortals, in our flesh suits, on planet Earth,

We must operate within the constraints of our "allotted time."

Our Allotted Time?

So, how much time is that?

Yes, we are free moral agents.

Made in the image & likeness of our Heavenly Father.

But, real freedom has a price, you see.

A price to be paid by you & me.

Therefore, as we function from day to day

We should vow to do what He says

Do what we were created to do

And get it done in "Our Allotted Time."

"YOUR SMILE"

My child, my child,

Where is your smile?

I had a design in mind

When I created you

That blueprint does not include some of the things

That I see you do.

Unnecessary are most of the struggles you go through.

I need you to read the notes I left on file

And let them be your guide.

My Father & I,

We see the tears you cry,

But tell me my child,

Where is your smile??

"DECISIONS"

When the time comes for me to make a choice

I stop, look, and listen

For HIS all knowing voice

Ever so faithfully

HE's always there for me

To guide my decision making

That I find myself undertaking

And, as long as I adhere

To "GOD'S" voice in my ear

I can never lose

For the right decision

I WILL CHOOSE.

"I SPEAK"

With your back up against a wall

You grab hold to anything to prevent the fall

Then you start digging in with your hips,

As you see yourself losing your grip

But, just when seemingly all hope is lost

In walks "The Big Boss"

Such a triumphal entrance he makes

Overwhelmed with His presence, I start to shake

The brightness of His Glory

Illuminates the room with light

And darkness is blitzed out of sight.

Now, I'm feeling love and

I'm feeling joy & peace

I am no longer that little lost, lonely sheep

I'm feeling strong

Oh y e a h , this is where I belong.

As King David said in Psalms 18:29

I can run through a troop

And you see that wall my back was upon

I just leaped over it !!!

Romans 8:31 says

If God be for you

Who can be against you?

I say to you :

When you see the odds stacking up against me

My brother & my sister, lose the doubt

A N D

NEVER make the mistake of counting me out

Instead, what you can do is

Count me "All"in."

I'm reminded of the Psalmist David

Psalms 116 :10 & Apostle Paul in 2nd Corinthians 4:13

And I believed, therefore I speak

Believe it, then speak it.

So what am I speaking?

I speak "Life".

A life that represents Christ

Thats the life I want to live.

A life that makes God proud.

And, I speak

Abundant living,

Because, the way I see it is

God does not divide,

He MULTIPLIES !!!!

Multiplication....

God's got the copyright on it.

I say "don't shine the spotlight on me"

Let us combine our lights and use them

To lead God's people back to Christ.

I believe, therefore I speak ....

"FELLOWSHIP"

Come one, come all

No gathering in the hall

Come on in

Take a load off your feet

Sit yourself down and have a seat

Listen to this compound word from my lips

"F-e-l-l-o-w-s-h-i-p

Let's shout it together

F e l l o w s h i p !!!!

Yeah, that's it

Singing & dancing & praising our Lord

Forget about the weather

We're on this ship together

Can I get a glory hallelujah

Or an "Amen" from the men

Together we stand,

Do I hear a " yes we can " ...

But divided...

WE ALL FALL.

Now I'm not concerned

With how you perform

What's important to me

Is this gathering of Family.

I can't help but smile

Like an innocent child

As I see the expectation

And, and, I can feel the excitation

In this great congregation !!!!!

So happy to be here

Sitting by you dear

And as far as my eyes can see

Nothing but FA-Mi-LY!!!!!!!!

Thank you very much

"ALMOST"

I want to raise a worldwide "Toast"

From coast to coast

I want to tell you about Almost.

For too many years,

Almost has kept me from facing my fears

Let's propose a toast, to Almost.

Almost loves to hang around

When I climb up, he pulls me back down,

A friend to the end ???

Let's raise a toast, to Almost.

Even when I throw a fit,

Almost, never quits !

So many tears I've cried

Lord knows I've tried

But "Almost" stays right by my side,

Let's give a sigh, as we lift our cups high, to Almost.

Nearly,

Not exactly,

All but,

Slightly short of my goal.

These are but a few, of the words I've been told.

Awwh, but what a party that I have planned,

To celebrate my main man,

This year of my life

Almost, becomes a ghost

But not before I raise my final toast, to Almost.

Now listen up, Almost

As a silent partner, you speak too loud,

And this day, I stand proud

As I raise this Omega toast

To you, my lifelong companion,

AKA, Mr. Almost.

To the fear, called "failure"

I fail, to continue to walk in fear.

To "almost made it"

Listen up, I've already succeeded.

To "nearly there"

No, no, I have arrived.

To the "mountains" blocking

In the mighty, matchless name of Jesus,

My Lord & Savior,

I Rise, so High over you !!!

Truth be told,

Almost, you are some kind of bold,

All these years pretending to be my friend

But in actuality,

You've been blocking me

From my expected end.

Now I encourage myself in the Lord....

I am somebody !

I am a child of the King !

I walk by faith, not sight !

I can do all things through Christ who strengthens me !

If God be for me, don't matter who's against me !

Yes, yes, Almost

You've been such a close friend

But this day I tell you our relationship "END"....

In closing, I know you've heard the phrase "it's so hard,

to say goodbye"

Well, it's a LIE

Adios amigo, ciao, au revoir, arrivederci !!!!!!!

"PAPER MESSAGES"

Jehovah Jireh has placed so many messages inside of me

Then He compelled me to deliver them to thee

Now I know, that He knows, I'm no preacher

Nor do I have a great ministry

I'm just Lil 'ole imperfect me.

A mere thought passed through my mind

I've got no tools to use for this great undertaking

But, God says

There'll be no escaping,

Use the pen & paper.

Guess I forgot during that brief millisecond of time

God hears the unspoken thoughts of the mind.

"PRESSURE"

Pressure of this life,

Is getting me down,

Instead of a smile,

All I do is frown.

Frowns change to sighing,

Sighing to crying,

When I look in the mirror,

It looks like I'm dying.

Man 'o man, I can't continue this way,

GOD, I need your help,

And I need it today.

If I step up my belief,

Will I get some relief,

If I call out to you in prayer,

Will You really be there?

"MANAGEMENT"

Listen up staff:

Right now I'm the announcer

Not the bouncer

I know how to play rough

I was built road tough

But as your coach

I use the "nice" approach

Now, don't make me change my game

I'll have y'all kneeling, saying my name

And if I didn't mention

I know how to make you pay attention

So respect me for who I am

To you, I am the man

With "your" plan

I can be the reason you stay

Or with one word,

I can make you Go Away

Just keep up with this hate

And we will SEPARATE !

"THE FIFTIETH YEAR"

During this year of Jubilee

I wait with expectancy

For what God has for me

While you're waiting on your sacred 40 acres

You gotta remember promises spoken

Are easily broken

Of course I'm speaking of promises made by man

Ohhhhhhhhh, but, that which is promised to us by God,

I'm talking about God, the Father,

Who gave, His Son

For our re- demp- tion !!!

Promises from Him, are for real, they are for sure.

And on that you can depend

Just keep looking up to Him.

"I CAN'T BREATHE"

Help me somebody please,

I can't breathe.! Anybody,

Anywhere,

Gotta be somebody out there, Hear my plea,

I can't breathe!

Our ancestors screamed, while praying on their knees,

and here I am today, saying,

I can't breathe!

I can't breathe!

I can't breathe! Help me somebody please,

I can't breathe!! How many more years?

Do we have to live with the fear,

I say the fear,

the fear,

Crying out through our tears, screaming

I can't breathe! Help me, somebody please, because

I can't breathe,

I can't breathe!!Can you help me anybody,

"I Can't Breathe!!"

www.ingramcontent.com/pod-product-compliance
Ingram Content Group UK Ltd.
Pitfield, Milton Keynes, MK11 3LW, UK
UKHW061622240426